aregivers,

...ers are designed to provide enjoyable reading experiences, as well as opportunities to develop vocabulary, literacy skills, and comprehension. Here are a few ways to support your beginning reader:

- Talk with your child about the ideas addressed in the story.

- Discuss each illustration, mentioning the characters, where they are, and what they are doing.

- Read with expression, pointing to each word. You may want to read the whole story through and then revisit parts of the story to ensure that the meanings of words or phrases are understood.

- Talk about why the character did what he or she did and what your child would do in that situation.

- Help your child to connect with characters and events in the story.

Remember, reading with your child should be fun, not forced. Each moment spent reading with your child is a priceless investment in his or her literacy life.

Gail Saunders-Smith, Ph.D

STONE ARCH READERS

are published by Stone Arch Books
151 Good Counsel Drive, P.O. Box 669
Mankato, Minnesota 56002
www.stonearchbooks.com

Library of Congress Cataloging-in-Publication Data
Crow, Melinda Melton.
    Truck buddies / by Melinda Melton Crow ; illustrated by Ronnie Rooney.
    p. cm. — (Stone Arch readers)
    ISBN 978-1-4342-1625-0 (library binding)
    ISBN 978-1-4342-1756-1 (pbk.)
    [1. Dump trucks—Fiction. 2. Trucks—Fiction.] I. Rooney, Ronnie, ill. II. Title.
PZ7.C88536Tr 2010
[E]—dc22

                                    2008053406

Summary: Dump Truck wants to play, but all the other trucks are working.
See if Dump Truck finds something else to do.

Creative Director: Heather Kindseth
Graphic Designer: Hilary Wacholz

Reading Consultants:
Gail Saunders-Smith, Ph.D
Melinda Melton Crow, M.Ed
Laurie K. Holland, Media Specialist

Printed in the United States of America in Stevens Point, Wisconsin.
062010
005847R

The little skunk is a friend of the truck pals.
Every time you turn the page, look for it.
Can you find the little skunk?

TRUCK BUDDIES

written by Melinda Melton Crow

illustrated by Ronnie Rooney

STONE ARCH BOOKS
MINNEAPOLIS   SAN DIEGO

This is Green Truck.
This is Dump Truck.
This is Blue Truck.

Dump Truck wants to play.

Dump Truck sees Blue Truck.

"Will you play with me?"
asks Dump Truck.

"No. I'm too busy," says
Blue Truck.

Dump Truck sees Green Truck.

"Will you play with me?"
asks Dump Truck.

"No. I'm too busy," says
Green Truck.

Dump Truck goes away.

"Who will play with me?"
asks Dump Truck.

Blue Truck and Green Truck
see their sad friend.

"You can help us work,"
says Green Truck.

"Then we can play," says
Blue Truck.

Dump Truck is happy to help!

STORY WORDS

truck	play	help
dump	busy	work

Total Word Count: 99

Follow your favorite truck pals as they learn about the open road.